GRANDPA JAKE AND THE GRAND CHRISTMAS

❄ ❄ ❄

MILDRED AMES

HBJ Harcourt Brace Jovanovich, Inc.
Orlando Austin San Diego Chicago Dallas New York

As a part of HBJ TREASURY OF LITERATURE, 1993 Edition, this
edition is published by special arrangement with Charles Scribner's
Sons, an imprint of Macmillan Publishing Company.
Grateful acknowledgment is made to Charles Scribner's Sons, an
imprint of Macmillan Publishing Company, for permission to reprint
Grandpa Jake and the Grand Christmas by Mildred Ames. Copyright
© 1990 by Mildred Ames.
Cover illustration copyright © 1990 by Patricia Mulvihill.
Printed in the United States of America
ISBN 0-15-304617-1
2 3 4 5 6 7 8 9 10   059   96   95   94   93

For Hannah Sampson and Bill

Contents

GRANDPA JAKE AND THE GRAND CHRISTMAS

❄ 1 ❄

Grandpa Jake

"I don't see why you don't make Lizzie do a better job of cleaning this house." Aunt Mary Margaret has a voice like chalk screeching up a blackboard. Her finger carves a path through the dust atop our Majestic radio. She holds up the same finger, blackened now. Papa, Cissy, and I stare at it in guilty silence.

It is a Sunday afternoon. None of us expected to see her so soon after Thanksgiving. Finally Papa says, "Lizzie does enough. I don't believe in turning a twelve-year-old into a housemaid."

I give him a startled look. Aunt Mary Margaret's visits are like inspections. If Cissy and I say mean things about her afterwards, Papa always defends her. I suppose that's because she's his younger sister. I'd do the same for Cissy. Sometimes, anyhow.

"Then I don't see why you don't hire someone to come in and clean for you," Aunt Mary Margaret declares.

"We have our own ways," Papa says. "Strangers want to change things around. Besides, a little dust never killed anybody."

Papa does not tell her that we can't afford to hire anyone. He is a mason who builds the most beautiful brick and stone walls you ever saw. But work is scarce right now because there is a depression. Without jobs and money, people can't put up the buildings that need the skills of Papa's trade.

Uncle Walter, Aunt Mary Margaret's husband, is a butcher with his own shop. He makes good money because people always have to eat. Papa says that he and Aunt Mary Margaret don't understand about people being out of work. Lazy, they call them. That's why we never let on that we're late with the rent each month. Papa says these are our own hardships and nobody else's business.

But I have my own worries today that are a lot more important than a little dust. I have a notice from Miss Pontchartrain, my dancing teacher, saying that, starting in January, she is raising the price of Cissy's and my dancing lessons. I dread showing it to Papa. I'm afraid he'll say we can't afford lessons anymore. If that happens, I don't know what I'll do. My long-term goal in life is to become a prima ballerina.

Both Aunt Mary Margaret and Papa say that's just a pipe dream, so I don't talk about it anymore. Besides, she is much more interested in good housekeeping anyhow. She says now, "I don't see why you don't remarry, Joseph." (Everyone else calls Papa Joe.) "The girls need a mother, and this place needs a—" She glances around the room, her eyes scouring the kitchen sink, whisking crumbs from the oilcloth on the table, and doing battle with the stubborn stains on the linoleum. "Well, it needs the touch of a woman."

"We're all right the way we are," Papa says. "Don't fret about us. You've got enough to worry about with your own brood."

Her own brood is the four cousins Cissy and I could do very well without.

She sighs to let us know she agrees with Papa about her heavy burden. Then her attention turns to the baking dish she has brought with her. "I thought you'd enjoy what's left of the Indian pudding. I can't imagine how you forgot to take it with you on Thanksgiving. You know I always give you what's left."

Cissy glances at me with a screwed-up face that leaves no doubt about what she thinks of Aunt Mary Margaret's Indian pudding. I silently agree with her. Every Thanksgiving it is the same. We all have to choke down a dish of it in the name of what Aunt Mary Margaret calls *tradition.* Then, lucky us, we get what's left.

"I'll put it in the icebox," I say quickly, afraid she may take that chore upon herself. Our forgotten leftovers and the way we cram everything around the cake of ice are surely good for a long lecture.

I take the dish to the hall, where we keep our box for the iceman's convenience. Before I put the pudding inside, the waxed paper cover comes loose and I have a glimpse of our unasked for bounty. Quickly, I shove it to the back and close the door.

As I return to the kitchen, Papa is saying, "Thanks for having us for Thanksgiving, Sis. It means a lot to the girls."

Aunt Mary Margaret says, "I think children need tradition. We'll expect you for Christmas, too."

Papa says, "Good of you."

Cissy and I exchange sick glances.

Soon after Aunt Mary Margaret leaves, Cissy says to Papa, "I don't want to go there for Christmas."

"We always go there," Papa says as though it's a law.

They live on the other side of town, so we take the bus over on Christmas Eve and spend the night. The next morning we open presents with our cousins. We give each of them one from the two of us. They give each of us one from the four of them. Their side gets four and ours gets two. That's never seemed quite fair to me. Papa says I mustn't think that way.

"Couldn't we just stay home this year?" I ask him.

"Your aunt's feelings would be hurt. And she's right. Tradition is important." He thinks about it some more. "Besides, we'd have to have a tree and the trimmings. And then there's Christmas dinner to think about. . . . On top of all that, we'd still have to buy presents for the rest of the family. No, we just can't afford it."

I think to myself, we could if we didn't buy all those presents. Especially the expensive kind Papa chooses for Aunt Mary Margaret's family. He says it's the least we can do to pay them back for having us for family holidays. It's my opinion, though, that he doesn't want them to know how little we have.

Through with the subject, Papa makes a quick check of the cupboard. "Lizzie, you forgot to get tea when you went to the store for me."

"I didn't forget. You didn't give me enough money."

"Oh," he says, then shrugs. "Oh, well, I'll just go next door to the Hanlons and borrow some."

I make a quick note in my mind to pay back the Hanlons later. Papa has so much on his mind these days with our money worries that he sometimes forgets little things like that.

While he is gone, I think of how to broach the subject of more expensive dance lessons. There is no easy way. I know he is straining to pay for them now.

I put the whole thing out of my mind as I check the pantry to see what we have in the house for supper. There are two cans of Franco-American spaghetti, one of peas, and another of sardines."

"What are we having?" Cissy asks.

"Franco-American."

"Oh, boy! My favorite. I could eat it everyday."

"Thanksgiving and Christmas too?" I ask, joking.

"Especially Thanksgiving and Christmas," she says very seriously.

"Maybe Aunt Mary Margaret will serve it this year, but don't count on it."

Cissy snorts, "I don't want to go there anyhow! I hate their old house, and I hate that old Sean. He pinched me all day when no one was looking."

Sean is closest to her age, seven going on eight. He is not my favorite person. Maureen, thirteen, is even less my favorite. She always takes me into her room to show off all her new clothes. Then she tells me about how she wears makeup to school and smokes cigarettes. If I say I don't believe her, she says, "Who cares? You're just a baby anyhow."

Last Thursday she said, "If you want to know what I want for Christmas"—I didn't—"I'll tell you. I want angora mittens and a matching beret."

So do a lot of people. Except me. I want a pink sweater and a single strand of pearls. But in her own words, *Who cares?* I have to admit, though, she stands a better chance of getting her wish than I do mine.

I say to Cissy now, "Want to or not, I'm afraid we'll have to go there for Christmas."

"Why?"

"Because it's what families do."

"But we're not a family—you, me, and Papa. Sean says we're not. He says nobody's a family unless there's a mama."

Cissy wasn't quite two when Mama died. She doesn't remember her the way I do. I remember warm hugging arms, soft lips, gentle hands, a cozy lap, and the nice smell of April Showers toilet water. For a moment I agree with Sean. We are not quite a family. Then I say, "Sean doesn't know what he's talking about. Of course we're a family—you, me, and Papa."

"I still don't want to go."

I know just how she feels. I picture our own house with our own Christmas tree and carols playing on the radio, and maybe even the pink sweater with the single strand of pearls. And no Indian pudding. Only at Christmastime it's plum pudding, which is even worse. I sigh. "I'm afraid there's no getting out of it."

As we ponder our dismal fate, the doorbell rings. Thinking Papa has forgotten his key, I go to answer it. Instead of Papa, a stout, well-dressed elderly man stands outside. Thick, wavy gray hair pokes out from beneath a fedora he wears at a jaunty angle. A battered satchel sits near his feet.

"Well, saints preserve us," the man says in a thick Irish brogue, "would you be Elizabeth?"

No one ever calls me Elizabeth. "Lizzie," I say, wondering if he has the wrong house.

"Elizabeth—named for your grandma, rest her soul," he exclaims, and I think he hasn't heard me. "And a fine young lady you are, all grown up like."

I don't know what to say, so I just stare at him.

He gives a hearty laugh. "Well, now, have you got a big hug for your grandpa Jake?"

Again I just stare. My grandparents died years ago.

❋ 2 ❋

Swan Lake

"Did you tell your father they're raising the price of your dancing lessons?" Tess asks as we walk home from school together.

"Not yet," I say. Tess (short for Theresa) Huminska is my best friend. She understands how I feel about ballet because she has a long-term goal, too. Someday she wants to become a famous aviator like Amelia Earhart. "I would have told him last night, but I didn't have a chance with my grandfather there. They had so much to talk about."

Tess, toothpick skinny and very blond, shakes her head in wonder. "Imagine having a grandfather all these years and not even knowing."

"None of us did. My father and my aunt thought he was dead because they never heard from him."

"Did he say why?"

"He said it's a long story, and he never was a letter writer anyhow, and besides, there were some who turned his children's minds against him, and not being here, he couldn't very well prove them wrong."

"Why did he come back now?"

"He says he's getting old, and he wants to put things to rights."

"Do you like him?"

"I don't know. He has this funny Irish brogue, but outside of that he seems all right. To tell the truth, I haven't given it much thought because I've been so worried about my dancing school problems."

"What'll you do if you have to quit?"

"I'll die, that's all!"

Always practical, Tess says, "I don't think so, but you won't be able to reach your short-term goal."

Tess and I long ago agreed that it is important to have goals, both short and long term. My short-term goal is to dance Clara in *The Nutcracker,* our dancing school's traditional Christmas presentation. I was hoping to get the part this year, but it went to Mabel Dennis. I got the Sugar Plum Fairy instead. I was really disappointed because I'm better than Mabel. But she has taken lessons longer. Miss Pontchartrain always considers that. *Next year,* I tell myself. Then I wonder if there will even *be* a next year.

Tess says, "I was kinda surprised when your father let Cissy take lessons too. I mean, because of the cost and all."

"They were only introductory lessons—twenty-five cents—or he wouldn't have done it. And it was only because her teacher said if she didn't start coming out of her shell, she might have real problems later. You know how shy Cissy is, how she keeps to herself. She won't even try to make friends at school."

"Funny, she's not shy around me."

"I know. We didn't even suspect it was a problem until the teacher told us. 'Cissy is painfully shy,' she said. She thought it might do her good to get into some outside activity, especially something physical. What could be more physical than dancing? Especially tap, which is all she's taking."

"How come?"

"That's all the introductory lessons are for. Besides, I had a hard enough time talking her into that."

"Is it doing anything for her?"

"Who knows? She's only been at it a few months." I, on the other hand, had started lessons when Mama was still alive. I suspect this is the only reason Papa lets me continue. He is always trying to do what he thinks Mama would have wanted. He has to be mother and father to us at the same time, he says. I guess that must be hard.

Tess says, "You know, you really don't look the part—like a ballerina, I mean."

I am indignant, this coming from Tess of all people. "How can you say that? I have a long neck, don't I? You have to agree I have a long neck. All ballerinas have long necks."

"I think they just look that way because they wear their hair up."

"So will I. I'm letting it grow now. When it's long enough, I'm going to part it in the middle and pull it back skin-tight behind my ears and knot it at the top. All ballerinas wear their hair that way."

"But yours is red. I think they all have black hair."

"I'll dye mine if I have to. Besides I'm working on developing my calves. That's more important than hair. You can tell someone's a ballerina just by looking at their calves. When mine are big enough, I'll look as much like one as anybody."

I must sound mad because Tess changes the subject. "I used to think you were going to be a toe dancer," she says. "I never even knew the word *ballet*. I used to call it toe dancing."

"Me too." I nod solemnly. "If it hadn't been for *Swan Lake*, I dread to think of what my long-term goal might have been. I started out just taking tap, you know. Of course, there's nothing wrong with tap dancers, but they're just nothing beside ballerinas. I mean, it's like comparing houseflies to butterflies."

For a moment I am again seated in the Mosque Auditorium, waiting for the curtain to open on a performance of *Swan Lake*. Miss Pontchartrain has a friend in the company who has given her complimentary matinee tickets for a few worthy students. She has reminded us repeatedly that we are, indeed, privileged. It is only as the ballet begins and the story unfolds that I start to believe her.

11

"Oh, Tess," I say, *"Swan Lake* was the turning point in my whole life." I had told her the story countless times: Prince Siegfried falls in love with Odette, queen of the swans. She and her court have been bewitched by the wicked magician, Rothbart, to live as swans from dawn to midnight. Siegfried is unsuccessful in freeing her. It is a lovely story with a bittersweet ending. The two must die to be together always.

The old Mosque Auditorium with its uncomfortable, half-broken seats just disappeared. There was only the magical onstage kingdom where handsome Siegfried, beautiful Odette, and all the lovely maidens in pristine white danced their hearts out, gliding, leaping, moving always with an effortless-seeming grace, the like of which I had never seen before. In my mind, I was on that stage with them, lost in an enchanted world of dance, where all is feeling and expression and beauty, a world I knew instantly I must belong to.

Tess says, "I wish I'd seen it with you. It must have been really something."

We are in front of my house now. She lives just across the street. The neighborhood is a far cry from the world of *Swan Lake.* I think of Tess whose family is on relief. Early tomorrow morning, before school starts, she will take her little brother's wagon and join the many other people who go to the food station for their allotment of groceries. I would die of shame if I had to do that.

Papa keeps saying, "We don't want to be like Tess's family and have to go on relief. We mustn't become charity cases." I have seen the food she returns with, though. What Papa does not realize is that people on relief eat better than we do.

"Are you coming over this afternoon?" Tess asks.

"I can't. My father says we have to take Aunt Mary Margaret's dish back. He wants Cissy and me to go with him. I think what he really wants, though, is moral support when he tells her about my grandfather."

"I should think she'd be real pleased."

"You don't know my aunt. She's never pleased about anything."

We say good-bye, and I start for my house, wondering when would be the best time to give Papa the notice from Miss Pontchartrain. The longer I put it off, the longer Clara stays within reach. And even Odette.

❆ 3 ❆

Aunt Mary Margaret

"The nerve of the man!" Aunt Mary Margaret says. "Gone eleven years and thinks he can walk back into our lives just like that. Well, not in mine, he can't. He is not welcome in this house. And you can tell him I said so."

Cissy, Papa, and I have returned the Indian pudding dish and broken the news about Grandpa Jake. Although it is late afternoon, all of our cousins are out except the baby, Rory, and he is napping.

Papa says, "He's still our father, Sis."

"A fine father *he* was! Disappearing for months, even years at a time. Always off wheeling and dealing, and none of it ever amounting to a row of pins."

"I know, I know," Papa says patiently. "But I can't turn him out now that he needs me."

14

"Needs you! He's never needed any of us, including Mama. I'll never forget what he did to her. He killed her!"

Cissy and I, wide-eyed, take in every word, learning things we would otherwise never have known. But Grandpa Jake—a murderer?

Aunt Mary Margaret soon relieves my mind. "If he hadn't shirked his responsibilities, she'd still be alive. But no, she put us first and worked her fingers to the bone in a miserable cafeteria to support us. That's what killed her. And it's him I blame."

"There's no changing the past," Papa says.

"And there's no forgetting it either! No, I want no part of him with his grand notions and promises. I don't remember one that he ever kept."

Papa says, "It's all water over the dam. Besides, he's an old man. He's got to be changed. Can't see how he can hurt anyone now."

"You mark my words, he'll find a way. Your trouble, Joseph, is you're just like Mama—soft. She always took him back. And he always did the same thing to her all over again."

"Who's soft? Doing your duty doesn't make a person soft," Papa says. "You weren't the only one he hurt, you know."

It is my opinion that Papa is not much more pleased than my aunt to have Grandpa Jake here, but Papa is different from her. If you asked her what was the most important godly thing in the world, she would say *cleanliness.* If you asked Papa, he'd say *duty.*

15

"How long is he staying this time?" Aunt Mary Margaret asks.

Papa shrugs. "I don't know. Maybe for good."

"Him of the restless feet?" She snorts. "Mark my words. He'll be off before you know it. And I hope he is!"

"You're sure you don't want to see him? At his age grandkids mean a lot, you know."

Aunt Mary Margaret's nose shoots straight up in the air. "As far as I'm concerned, I have no father. And my children have no grandfather. I will not have that man in our house or in our lives."

Papa sighs. "All right. I'll tell him somehow."

We leave soon after. On the bus trip home, Cissy whispers to me, "They have the mama, but *we* have the grandpa."

As if that made everything better than even.

✳ 4 ✳

The Frenchman's Curse

"Even when she was knee-high to a grasshopper, 'twas a cake of ice Mary Margaret had for a heart. And that's the straight of it," Grandpa Jake says.

Papa has just told him the bad news. We are all in the kitchen, Cissy at the table drawing paper dolls, me doing homework, Papa standing in the doorway, looking as if he can't wait to escape.

Grandpa Jake is in shirt sleeves at the coal stove, stirring a pungent-smelling dish he is making for our supper. Lone Star chili, he calls it. He dips out a spoonful, blows on it, and tastes. Grinning at Cissy and me, he gives a contented sigh. "Ah, a dish fit for all the saints in heaven!" he declares.

Even though the odor is not exactly enticing, my mouth still waters.

Papa shifts uncomfortably. "I'm sorry, Jake, but that's the way she is."

I think how strange it is to call your father by his first name.

Grandpa Jake says, "Well, 'tis her loss." He returns his attention to his cooking as if that is far more important.

"I'll be in the dining room if anyone wants me," Papa says. "Got to go over our budget for the month."

I wonder if he is saying that for Grandpa Jake's benefit. I'm sure Papa is worried that we have one more mouth to feed now.

When he disappears, Grandpa Jake says, "Can you guess where I got this recipe?"

Cissy and I say we can't.

"Got it from an old cowpoke down in Texas, I did."

"What were you doing there?" I ask.

"Drillin' for oil, darlin'. What else would a body be doin' in Texas?"

I have no idea. "Did you find any?"

"Did I find any? Just the biggest gusher you ever laid eyes on." He stares off into another time. "Ah, a beauty 'twas—black gold."

I wonder if he is rich. Anxiously I ask, "What happened?"

He gives a long sigh. "Cheated by a thievin' partner, that's what happened. One of the devil's own, that man was." He shakes his head. " 'Tis many a fortune I've made and lost." Then he grins, and his bright blue eyes sparkle. "Ah, well—easy come, easy go, I always

18

say." He steps over and ruffles Cissy's red hair. "And what do *you* always say, darlin'?"

Her voice serious, Cissy says, "That's what I always say too."

He gives her shoulder an affectionate pat. "You're a Mahoney, sure enough. Would you believe I once had hair as red as your own and Lizzie's?"

Papa and Aunt Mary Margaret too have our color hair. But Grandpa Jake's wavy mop is gray, almost white. Cissy giggles.

"Well, I did, you know. And what about your cousins—carrot tops too?" he asks.

"They're blonds—all of them," I say. "Papa calls them towheads. He says they take after Uncle Walter, the Polish side of the family."

"Blond, are they? Well, they're no grandchildren of mine then. Even your grandma, rest her soul, had hair as black as ink."

Excited, Cissy says, "You're *our* grandpa, nobody else's—not Sean's or Maureen's or Junior's or Rory's—just ours. Right, Grandpa Jake?"

"Right! From this moment on, I disown the lot of them. Blonds, indeed!"

Cissy and I exchange big smiles.

A little later we all try his Lone Star chili. It is quite a shock. Every bite bites back. We wash it down with plenty of water.

After dinner, while Papa works on his budget, Grandpa Jake helps Cissy and me with the dishes. All the while he tells us exciting stories about the West.

"There was the time I was within a breath of findin' the richest gold mine in the country—out in California 'twas, way up in the Sierra Nevada," he says.

"What happened?" I ask.

" 'Tis a long story." He settles in a chair at the kitchen table.

Cissy and I leave the clean dishes to drain as we join him. "I love long stories," she says.

"Ever heard of the Frenchman's cursed mine?" he asks. Cissy and I shake our heads, and he continues. "Seems back in the gold-rush days, this Frenchy, prospectin' out there, found himself a mine of gold so pure and rich not even the Spanish explorers lookin' for El Dorado could have imagined it." He stares into space as though envisioning the gold-paved streets of that city. It is only a legend, I've read.

"What happened?" I ask, to prod him on.

His eyes clear. "The Frenchy was murdered for the gold he brought back."

"What about the mine?"

"The location of all that riches he took to his death. Folks say that before he died he put a curse on the mine. If he couldn't enjoy the gold, no one else would. And many's the man hunted for the place but"—he pauses for the dramatic effect of his next words—"each and every last one of them met"—again he pauses—"well, suffice to say, the cruelest of fates."

In sparing us the details, he has left my mind free to fill in its own pictures of men dismembered by mountain lions or locked in fatal combat with snarly bears who bite off their heads or other tender parts. "What happened to *you?*" I ask, not sure I want to hear.

"Well, darlin', I met this old prospector who claimed he'd found a map of the Frenchman's mine. Found it in his dead partner's effects, he told me. All that was standin' between him and a fortune was a grubstake. And that, I regret to say, I supplied."

"What's a grubstake?" Cissy asks, and I explain that it's money for food and tools and whatever is needed.

Grandpa Jake continues. "Well, now, off we go up into the mountains, followin' the path marked on the map. Summer, 'twas, with warm, beautiful weather. We camped in the high country, sleepin' under the stars, breathin' in all that fine air. What could go wrong on so perfect a trip, says I."

Cissy and I wait breathlessly for him to tell us.

"After four days and nights we are close to the X that marks the mine on the map. And aren't we just the happy ones!"

We listen in rapt silence.

"And within a breath of our goal, up comes a storm, the likes of which I never hope to see again. The skies open up and let out a flood of water. All the time lightnin' bursts like bombs over our heads, and thunder shakes the very ground beneath our feet. Says I to myself, 'Sure we'll wash clear off this old mountain.' "

"What did you do?"

"The two of us took to our heels. You'd have thought the devil himself was chasin' us. Lookin' for a dry cave, we were—anyplace out of the holocaust." He shakes his head solemnly. " 'Twas not to be."

"What happened?" Cissy and I say in unison.

"Like a bolt out of hell, lightnin' shoots down and strikes the earth only a spittin' distance from me. With a deafenin' roar in my ears I turn around, and what do you think I find?"

We shake our heads.

"A sight to make the hair stand straight up on your head. A fiery current shoots through the old prospector, turning him into a creature right out of hell—electrocuted, he was—burned to a crisp before my very eyes!"

Cissy and I gasp.

"Before my eyes, mind you. And not a blessed thing can I do. Ah, I tell you, there's not an Irishman alive who doesn't recognize the voice of the devil when he hears it."

"Oooh," I say, "the Frenchman's curse!"

"The very same." Grandpa Jake looks devoutly righteous as he says, "Well, I tell you, no gold is worth a man's life. I swore to God I'd have none of it."

"What happened to the map?" I ask. After all, treasure maps are the stuff of dreams.

"You'd never believe it, but that piece of paper was washed clean. Whether by God or the devil it don't much matter. What does matter is I turned my back on a fortune the likes of which no king has ever known.

And I'll tell you somethin' else. I'm the better man for it."

Cissy and I, both dazzled, exchange delighted glances. What a noble man he is, our grandfather. Cissy whispers to me, "Grandpa Jake is better than listening to the radio." I have to agree.

✳ 5 ✳

Papa's Pipe Dream

The following day, after school, I find Papa alone in the kitchen. Cissy gets home later than I. Grandpa Jake, Papa tells me, has gone to the drugstore for shaving needs. I have no excuse to keep Miss Pontchartrain's notice to myself any longer.

Papa studies it carefully. At length he says, "It's costing a dollar a week for the two of you now. This is almost double that. She must think money grows on trees."

"Miss Pontchartrain says she charges less than everyone else, and she's losing money."

Still staring at the notice, Papa says, "Well, maybe it's just as well. Dancing lessons were fine when times were better. Right now they're a luxury we can't afford."

24

No wonder I'd waited so long to tell Papa. This was exactly what I'd expected—a few simple words that were destroying my whole life. "How can I hope to become a prima ballerina without lessons?" I cry in desperation. "You need years of study and practice."

"Oh, Lizzie, I thought you'd put that foolishness out of your mind long ago."

"Well, I haven't. And it's not foolishness," I say stubbornly, blinking back tears.

He says impatiently, "That's pie in the sky. You know how I feel about that. Sure, at your age kids have a lot of wild notions, but sooner or later they have to be realistic. You'll find out when you grow older."

The problem is I don't think of ballet as a wild notion. I say, "You just don't understand. How could you when you've never had any—any wild notions."

"That's not quite true. I've had my share. Every kid does. Why, I remember the time when I used to tell everybody I was going to join the circus." He shakes his head and smiles at his foolishness. "And later I thought I'd become—" He breaks off. "Well, it doesn't matter. Life doesn't always offer choices."

"You'd become what?" I persist.

"Oh, just more foolishness." His smile looks forced now. He says with great exaggeration, "I was going to be a world-famous architect."

So Papa had had his dream, too. "Maybe you could have been if you'd tried."

He dismisses the idea with, "Aaah—nothing but a pipe dream. And you know how I feel about those. The only purpose they serve is to make you discontent with what you have."

I wonder if Papa isn't discontent anyhow. When he was sixteen, he apprenticed to his mother's brother to learn masonry. Aunt Mary Margaret said that, with no father in the house to bring in money (and it is hard for me right now to think of Grandpa Jake as that absent father), he felt it was expected of him. I know Papa likes what he does, but all the same, I don't see how he can help regretting what might have been.

"Miss Pontchartrain says I have talent, Papa," I say.

He sighs, sounding as if he has run out of ways to make me understand. Finally he says, "Lizzie, I know how much you enjoy dancing. Believe me, I do. I like dancing myself."

He doesn't understand. He's talking about something entirely different.

"Did I ever tell you how I met your mother?"

Now he's changing the subject. And yes, he's told me many times.

"She was a high school graduate, you know."

Papa is always so proud of that. He left school early to go to work. He loves to tell the story about how they met shortly before she graduated. It was at a local dance studio that no longer exists. All of the high school kids went there on Saturday mornings to learn the fox-trot and the Charleston and get dates for the prom. Papa and one of his friends went as a lark,

26

wanting to get in on some of the high school fun he'd missed. There he'd met Mama. He wound up taking her to the prom, where they fox-trotted and Charlestoned all night. Usually I love to hear him talk about it. Today I have no patience for reminiscing. "I know the story, Papa. And dancing that way is just not the same thing as wanting to do it for a career."

I can see he is all prepared to take the conversation down a pleasanter road, but my words stop him and bring him back to the present. Finally he gives a long sigh and says, "The simple truth is I just don't have the money for anything extra at the moment, Lizzie. You know how slow my work is in winter. I have one job coming along before Christmas, and after that, I just don't know."

I want to say that dancing is not something extra for me, but I know that won't change anything.

He looks deeply into my eyes. "You have to understand, Lizzie, that right now it's as much as I can do to put food in our stomachs and keep a roof over our heads. I just don't have a penny to spare—not a penny."

For a moment I share his despair. And I am flattered that he thinks me mature enough to confide in. Oh, what a selfish daughter I am! An ingrate, worried only about myself. I vow to work on all my shortcomings, to spend more time housecleaning and learning to cook, to make myself helpful in every way I can think of. In the next breath, I ask, "Can I keep on with lessons until January when the price changes? I'm supposed to dance in *The Nutcracker,* you know. Miss Pontchartrain is counting on me."

"I know." He smiles at me fondly. "Sure. Keep on until then."

Until then. After that?

All my noble intentions of a moment ago no longer feel so noble. Some people are comfortable wearing hair shirts, but I don't seem to be one of them. There has to be some way I can continue with my lessons. I intend to find it.

❆6❆

Grandpa Jake
Lets Us Down

"You can do it, Cissy," I say. "Start with your right
foot like this—" As usual, we are both early for our
dance classes, so I have been working with her on her
military tap.

In fact, ever since she started lessons, I have somehow wound up helping not only her, but everyone else
in her class. Her teacher, it seems, has another job and
only teaches dancing for the extra money. He usually
shows up late. In the meantime, his pupils, her age or
younger, run wild through the room, doing everything
but what they came there to do.

On Cissy's first day Miss Pontchartrain was at her
wit's end, screaming, "Why can't that man get here
earlier? What does he think I hired him for? I don't
have time for his classes and mine too!" Then she

spotted me with Cissy. "Oh, am I ever glad to see you, Elizabeth. Maybe you can do something with these kids until Art gets here."

"Do what?" I said, glancing at a shrieking group playing a violent game of tag.

"Well, I don't know. Show them some steps. You've had enough tap and acrobatics lessons to know how to help them keep busy." I opened my mouth to object, but she stopped me with, "Please, Elizabeth, you'd be doing us all such a big favor." And she was off before I could do much about it.

That was how it had started. After that Miss Pontchartrain called upon me to work with the class whenever Art Patchen was late, which was just about always. I didn't really mind. The little kids were fun and not as much trouble as I'd expected. All I had to do was show Cissy a step, and they were upon me with pleas of *Show me too* or demonstrations followed by *Look at me. I can do it.* Or *Is this right?* The strange thing is that I've had a lot of success with everyone except Cissy. Maybe because she's my sister.

Cissy's trouble is she is so bashful she gets self-conscious. She imagines everyone is looking at her. The truth is the other pupils are so busy perfecting their own steps they have no interest in watching anyone else.

Except Ruthie Cornfield. She is about Cissy's age and has just started lessons. Today she stands close by, and her big black eyes take in Cissy's and my every move.

Cissy, put off by the clatter of so many feet tapping away over the polished floor, glances around nervously. Then she makes a feeble try at doing the step I've just shown her. Finally she says firmly, "I can't do it, Lizzie."

"Yes, you can. Here, I'll show you again. Now try to do it with me this time." As I begin, it is Ruthie who joins me with the clickety, click, click, click; clickety click, click, click that opens the dance.

"*I* can do it," Ruthie says importantly. She trots over to Cissy's side. "It's easy. See—" She begins again, awkward but persistent.

I expect Cissy to be put off. Instead, she is caught up in Ruthie's demonstration. "That's not right," Cissy says. "I can do it better than that. I'll show you."

To my surprise the two of them, far from perfect, are soon tapping away, so involved in each other's efforts that Cissy has obviously forgotten all the imaginary eyes on her.

"Good," I say. Cissy, it seems, just needed someone her own age, at her own level of skill, to make her feel less alone. "Now I'll show you the next step," I offer.

As I take the two of them through it, Miss Pontchartrain, along with Cissy's teacher, Art Patchen, comes in on us. I am reminded that I should be working at the *barre* in the room upstairs instead of helping beginners. "Gotta go," I tell the girls and start to hurry off.

Miss Pontchartrain stops me. "One moment, Elizabeth." She is a skinny woman, very theatrical, who

31

lives in leotards. She motions me aside and in her deep, almost masculine voice says, "I'm glad to see you're helping your sister."

My sister wasn't the only one I was helping, but I was sure Miss Pontchartrain knew that. Besides, how could I complain when I was doing something I enjoyed?

She went on with, "Art tells me he can't do much with her. She just doesn't show any interest."

"It's because she's so shy," I say.

"Well, she'll just have to get over that if she wants to take part in our beginners' number in next year's recital."

"I'm sure she will," I say, not sure at all.

A little later, during ballet class, it occurs to me that it really doesn't much matter. According to Papa, neither one of us will be here next year. Then I push the thought aside. Haven't I promised myself to find a way?

After class, Cissy and I wait outside the school, where Grandpa Jake has promised to meet us. "We'll go Christmas-wish shopping," he'd said last night. Cissy and I are really excited about it. The shops have such beautiful merchandise this time of year. With Grandpa Jake along, we will be able to go into the better ones. Alone we'd never dare.

We wait and wait. Cissy looks up and down the street, fidgeting impatiently, every minute thinking she's spotted Grandpa Jake coming along in the distance. Each time she is wrong. "Maybe he can't find Miss Pontchartrain's," she says.

The studio is on the corner of Main and State streets, the most findable place in town, I think. It isn't as if Grandpa Jake is some stranger. Besides, although it was once a store, there is a huge sign outside now. I don't think anyone could miss it.

The big clock on Main Street says we have waited forty minutes in the cold. Both of us are chilled through. "I think we'd better go home," I say. Then for Cissy's sake, I add, "I guess Grandpa Jake just couldn't find the place."

We are both so disappointed we trudge home in silence.

❄7❄

A Direct Line
to the North Pole

"Ah, 'tis the same old town," Grandpa Jake says, taking in Main Street.

He, Cissy, and I are finally on the Christmas-wish shopping trip he'd promised us. We have forgiven him for standing us up yesterday because it was all our mistake. When we'd confronted him later in the day and told him how long we'd waited, he'd looked at us blankly at first. Then his expression changed to deep concern.

"You poor loves, waitin' all that time, freezin' your toes off. And all because of me—all my fault."

We stared at him accusingly because, yes, it was his fault. "You said you'd meet us after dancing class," I said.

"So I did. But I understood that was tomorrow afternoon."

"Oh, no, Grandpa Jake—today."

"Today, was it? Well, now, there you go. That explains it. A clear misunderstandin'. I was that certain you meant tomorrow." He'd hung his head in pretend shame. "Do you suppose you have it in your hearts to forgive a thick Irishman?"

Of course we did. Anyone can make a mistake—although I still can't figure out what we'd said to mix him up like that.

But what does it matter? We're here now, and yesterday is forgotten. This afternoon Papa is working on a job he says may last a whole week. As for me, I have put aside my problems for the moment to show Grandpa Jake the town's Christmas decorations.

He shakes his head. "Now wouldn't you think after all this time they'd get themselves some new trimmin's?"

The street is festooned, from one side to the other, with shiny silver garlands, a little rusty now. Big red bells hang from the center and over the traffic. I think they are very pretty, but I say, "I guess they can't afford new because of the Depression."

Cissy says, "That's why Santa Claus brings us long underwear—because of the Depression."

Grandpa Jake says, "Underwear, is it?"

"Yes," says Cissy, sounding as though she means to educate him. "That's because Santa can only afford to leave one present. And we really need the underwear more than toys. Sean already had long underwear, so he got a fire engine. I didn't care, though. I didn't want a fire engine anyhow."

I could still see Cissy's face last Christmas morning as she opened the small, ribbon-tied box. There was no way the doll she wanted could fit inside something that flat.

Grandpa Jake says, "Well, now, I'll just have to have a talk with old Santy this year."

Cissy's eyes grow big. "Do you know Santa Claus?"

"Do I know Santy Claus?" he exclaims, sounding indignant. "Why, 'tis the best of friends we are, the two of us bein' about the same age, you know."

I have to smile. Give him a red suit and a white beard, and he might well be taken for Santa himself, I think. He already has the rosy cheeks, the twinkle in his eye, the pot belly, and the hearty laugh.

Cissy says, "Then I wish you'd tell him I'd rather not have long underwear this year. Lizzie can sew up the holes in my old."

"God love you, I'll tell him this very week," Grandpa Jake promises.

As we near J. M. Fried's department store, we can hear the Christmas carols that issue from a loudspeaker and carry up Main Street. Nearby a bonneted woman in a Salvation Army uniform stands over a pot waiting for people's change. Her tinkling bell mingles with the music.

"Well, now, if that don't give you the Christmas

spirit, I don't know what will," Grandpa Jake says. Then he points to J. M. Fried's window. "And speak of the devil, 'tis himself."

An animated Santa sits behind the glass, nodding his head and waving at us. His elves hammer and saw tirelessly, supposedly turning out all the toys displayed there. Although there is none outside, inside the window a gentle snow falls. As we watch, Cissy's nose presses against and clouds the glass. I'm sure she doesn't notice that the sparkly white carpet is only cotton sprinkled with glitter.

Grandpa Jake says, "Before we freeze off our toenails, let's have a look inside."

Inside J. M. Fried's? This is what we have looked forward to. With Grandpa Jake beside us, we don't have to be afraid to enter. Although I have noticed that his nice clothes are a bit frayed at the elbows, he still looks like a man of importance. We march bravely in beside him.

He says, "Well, now, what'll it be first?"

"Toyland," Cissy says.

"Toyland, is it? Good choice."

The elevator operator tells us we want the third floor. We pile into a full car, stuffy with the smells of wool and people, and pile out when the arrow points to "3."

Cissy is mostly interested in the dolls. "Don't touch them," I warn for the benefit of the clerk, a sour-looking woman. For a moment I am sure she has taken us for beggars and will surely banish us from this

37

elegant establishment. Then I remember we are with Grandpa Jake.

A few of the dolls sit on a counter, but most are behind on shelves. Cissy examines them all carefully with her eyes. Suddenly she points and says, "Oh, look." My eyes follow her finger to a small open trunk on one of the shelves. In one side is a Little Orphan Annie doll who, with her red hair, looks a lot like Cissy. On the other side are three party dresses.

Cissy says, "Oh, she's so cute."

Grandpa Jake says, "That one, is it?" He stares the salesclerk right in the eye. "We'll have a look at her."

The woman transfers doll and trunk from shelf to counter. She points out all the interesting features. The doll is a faithful copy of the cartoon character, right down to her shoes. The party dresses, of course, are gifts from the rich Daddy Warbucks. She goes on for some time.

Cissy and I listen as though struck dumb. The clerk has gone to so much trouble—and all for us. How will we ever live through the embarrassment of not buying the doll? I busy myself inventing all kinds of apologetic excuses. Maybe we can say Papa is elsewhere in the store, and we will run and get his permission. Then we will make our escape and never darken the doors of J. M. Fried's again.

While I am planning all this, Grandpa Jake says to the woman, "As fine a doll as ever I've laid eyes on, I'm thinkin'. 'Tis a happy little girl who'll find the likes of such under her Christmas tree."

"Oh, yes," Cissy agrees.

"And what a lucky thing it is that Santy is such a good friend of mine. I'll just make myself a note to be sure and tell him when I see him—in person, so to speak." He whips out a small book from an inside pocket and borrows a pencil from the clerk. As he starts to write, he says, "Now I want to be sure to get this right—one Annie doll—"

Cissy corrects him. "One Little Orphan Annie doll." He repeats her words to satisfy her. Then she adds anxiously, "Don't forget the trunk and party dresses."

"Indeed!" He jots down the important words. Then he winks at the clerk, who gives him a conspirator's smile. He returns the smile and says, "Sure it's a grand way you have with words, Miss."

The woman doesn't look at all sour now.

As we leave the toy department, Cissy whispers to me, "Did you hear that, Lizzie? Grandpa Jake's going to tell Santa Claus—in person!"

"I heard."

Cissy turns to Grandpa Jake. "Now we have to find a present for Lizzie. Then you can tell Santa in person about hers too."

Cissy is sure we now have a direct line to the North Pole. I wonder if I was ever so young.

❄8❄

A Pink Sweater and a Single Strand of Pearls

We take the elevator to the second floor of J. M. Fried's. I lead the way to the Young Miss sweater department because I know exactly what I want. And it isn't long underwear.

After all, I am in junior high school now. Some of my teachers even call me *Miss* Mahoney. And all of the girls who are anybody wear saddle shoes and go barelegged except for ankle socks. I have already told Papa I would die of shame if anyone saw me in long underwear. And, of course, they would. We have to take showers in gym class.

All he said was, "I will not have you going all winter with blue legs. It's not what your mother would have wanted. You'll at least wear stockings."

My stockings are lisle and ugly. And my shoes are

not saddle shoes but a pair of clunkers that Maureen refused to wear. But I figure if you can win one battle at a time, you're ahead.

The girl I admire most in school is Gloria Lacey. You can tell she is really somebody. It is December, and her parents still let her go with bare legs and anklets. Not only that, she wears the prettiest sweaters and skirts. And pearls. I heard her tell another girl that her mother always says there is nothing more ladylike and understated than a single strand of pearls. I was glad to learn that. It is my opinion that ballerinas should look ladylike and understated—a word I had not known before—both onstage and off.

Now I spot the sweater counter and lead the way. The clerk here is younger than the one in dolls. Her mouth works at a stick of gum that must be fresh because it gives off a wintergreen smell.

Grandpa Jake says to her, "We'd like to see somethin' in a nice sweater for this young lady." He points to me. "The best you've got."

"Pullover," I whisper to him. "Pink."

"Pink pullover," he says.

The clerk looks me up and down, her jaw going steadily. Then she reaches under the counter and comes up with a robin's-egg-blue sweater.

"Well, what do you think?" Grandpa Jake asks me.

"It's not pink," I whisper.

"It must be pink," he tells the girl.

Cissy says, "Pink is Lizzie's most favorite color in the whole world."

41

Quickly the clerk puts in, "With that hair? Oh, no." She reaches underneath again and comes up with moss green.

"Pink," I say timidly but loud enough for her to hear this time.

She shakes her head at my hopelessness. "You should always stick with cool colors. In fact, I have just the thing." She goes below again and this time bobs up with pale lavender.

Grandpa Jake looks at her, then at me.

"Pink," I say.

The clerk, chewing furiously now, whips around to a shelf behind her. From a neat pile of pinks, she jerks out one of my size and tosses it on the counter.

"Perfect," I murmur.

Grandpa Jake says, "Is that the best you have now?"

"In *pink,* yes," she says in a tone that suggests the quality is much superior in other colors.

"That's the one then." He glances down at Cissy. "I'll be tellin' Santy this very week."

She says, "You'd better write it down."

"Of course." He pulls out his little book and pretends to make a note in it.

The clerk frowns. "You mean you're not taking the sweater now?"

Grandpa Jake chuckles. "Have us do Santy's work for him, would you? Ah, that would never do."

She whisks the sweater away from us and makes a great show of folding and putting it back with the other pinks. Although she makes no comment, her gum cracking says it all.

Grandpa Jake asks me, "Wasn't there somethin' else you were wantin' from Santy?"

"A single strand of pearls," I tell him. "But that's easy to find. Woolworth's five-and-ten has lots of them."

"Then we'll just go have a look. How does that suit you, Miss Elizabeth Mahoney?"

"Everybody calls me Lizzie, Grandpa Jake."

"Lizzie, is it? Well now, just don't put up with it. Elizabeth was your sainted grandma's name. And a fine name 'tis—a name fit for queens. Never let them call you anythin' less."

He has just made my name sound very special, and I like that.

Cissy says, "I sure wish it would snow. That would make everything perfect."

Grandpa Jake says, "Well now, give it time." He makes a great show of studying the almost clear sky. Then he points to an unimportant little cloud. "See that? A good sign. I predict a nice snowfall by Christmas Eve."

As we make for Woolworth's, Grandpa Jake puts his arms around Cissy and me. He gives us both a big squeeze and says, "Och, it's a grand Christmas we'll be havin'."

❄ 9 ❄

Grandpa Jake's Promise

Name almost any spot in the United States and Grandpa Jake has been there. "Come over from the old country when I was a lad of nineteen, I did," he says. "Swore I'd see as much of this great land as I could before I'm under the sod. And that I've done."

Papa is at an Elks Club meeting. He says he keeps up his membership because it helps him get jobs. Grandpa Jake has the ironing board out in the kitchen. As he talks to Cissy and me, he runs the hot flatiron over a damp cloth that covers his best trousers. He says he is sharpening the crease. Tomorrow he plans to visit a friend he knew long ago when he lived here. He says he wants to look prosperous, and you don't look prosperous if you don't look neat. He cares a lot more about how he looks than Papa does.

As the iron sizzles and steams, Grandpa Jake says, "Ah, there's fortunes to be made all over the place. Never mind gold mines out in California or oil in Texas—land's the thing. That's where the money is. Just give me an honest partner with a bit of capital." He taps his head. "I'll supply the gray matter. And, between us, we'll soon be millionaires."

Cissy and I listen, enthralled.

I am at the table, working on a pot-holder mitten from material out of the scrapbag of our neighbor, Mrs. Hanlon. She has shown me how to sew and helped me cut out this pattern. The mitten will be Papa's Christmas present from Cissy and me. He is always burning himself when he uses the oven. I think he will be pleased because it is such a clever invention. I only wish I could come up with something to give Cissy. So far I don't even have an idea.

Grandpa Jake knows what I am doing. He glances at my work now and says, "Won't your pa be the proud one when he finds a grand present like that under your tree Christmas morning."

I say, "We aren't going to have a tree."

"And why not, I'd like to know?"

"Because we go to Aunt Mary Margaret's for Christmas."

Cissy and I pour out the whole story, with all our saved-up complaints. We shamelessly reveal our selfish selves, pining for dolls and pink sweaters. He is so easy to talk to. He does not chide us about duty and pride, the way Papa would.

45

When we finish, he exclaims, "Sure I've never heard the like. It's a Christmas of your own you should be havin' with a tree and all the trimmin's. What can the man be thinkin' of? Well, never you mind. I'll have a word with him."

I say, "It wouldn't matter about the tree anyhow. We don't have any ornaments to put on it."

"Ornaments? In my time we made our own."

"Out of what?" I ask.

"Why, out of popcorn, out of paper, out of anything we had. I'll show you how myself."

"When?" Cissy says anxiously.

"This very week. Tomorrow we'll start poppin' the corn." He gives his head a disapproving shake. "No ornaments, indeed!"

Cissy and I exchange hopeful glances.

"That will never do. Not if Jake Mahoney has anything to say about it. And I promise you he will. Ah, yes, you'll have your very own Christmas. And a grand one at that."

He makes it all sound so easy.

Later, when Cissy is in bed, I have a rare chance to talk to him alone. I am curious about the bad things Aunt Mary Margaret says about him, but I can't think of a polite way to ask about those. Instead, I say, "I never knew my grandmother—Papa's mama. What was she like, Grandpa Jake?"

"Oh, a saint, Lizzie. Why, I wasn't fit to kiss her

feet." He smiles impishly. "Or so she often told me—although not in those words."

That surprised me. "Does that mean she wasn't so nice?"

"Now I didn't say that. Although *nice* is not exactly the right word for a saint."

"Didn't she ever want to travel with you on your"—I didn't quite know what to call his long absences—"trips?"

He shakes his head. "And many's the time I asked her. But she'd have none of it. 'You've not got an adventurous bone in your whole body,' I'd often tell her. And what do you think she'd say?" He looked indignant.

"I don't know."

"She'd say, 'It's rainbows you're chasin', and I'll not live my life that way.' Then I'd say, 'We're all chasin' somethin'—better rainbows with a pot of gold at the end than a gold watch after a lifetime of drudgery.' But no, no rainbow chasin' for her."

He looks annoyed, as though he is reliving that argument, so I try to change the mood by joking. "Did you ever catch one?"

He looks puzzled. "Catch one? Oh, a rainbow, you mean." He smiles now. "You might say I've caught my share." Then his expression slowly changes, and his eyes glaze over. At length he says softly, almost to himself, "What she never understood was, for some, the chase *is* the rainbow."

47

Does that mean he doesn't care about the pot of gold? I wonder.

He seems suddenly aware of me and grins. "Saints are not always the easiest of people to live with, you know."

I think I must be a lot like Grandpa Jake, although, to me, the pot at the end is the important thing. At the moment I can't say much for my chances of reaching it though. "I guess I'm chasing rainbows, too," I say.

He studies me with interest. "Are you now? And what might yours be?"

I tell him about my long-term goal of becoming a prima ballerina, and about how Papa calls it a pipe dream, and about how my lessons must end with the new year because we can't afford them.

Grandpa Jake takes it all in, then says, "You're a bit like me, Elizabeth. To some of us life would have no meanin' without our dreams. And it's that sure I am you're one of those."

"Oh, I am, Grandpa Jake," I assure him. "I just wish I was like Cissy. She doesn't even want to take lessons."

"Doesn't she now?" He mulls over my words thoughtfully, then says, "Seems to me that just might be your answer."

I start to say I don't understand. In the next instant it comes to me so clear and simple I wonder why I haven't thought of it before. Of course. Papa is paying a dollar for the two of us right now, twenty-five cents for Cissy's lessons, seventy-five cents for mine. Starting next year, hers will be seventy-five cents, mine a dollar. If she quit, he wouldn't have to spend a penny more than he does now. After all, it was only the increase he had complained about. What a perfect solution!

"Grandpa Jake, you're wonderful," I say.

We smile at each other like a couple of conspirators.

"Will you come see me dance in *The Nutcracker*?" I ask. "It's on Saturday, the nineteenth."

"Would you be thinkin' I'd miss an important occasion like that? Why, I'll be there with bells on."

❄ 10 ❄

A Time for Forgiveness

I look up from the library book I am reading and say, "Papa, do you think it's right to leave Grandpa Jake all alone on Christmas Eve and Christmas Day while we're at Aunt Mary Margaret's?"

We are alone in the kitchen. Grandpa Jake is visiting his old friend. Cissy is asleep. I sit with my feet in the oven to warm them while Papa plays solitaire at the table.

Cards in hand, he pauses. "I've been thinking about the very same thing."

Papa's decisions always rest on which way he sees his duty. I feel I may be able to shift the balance to our side. "He'd be awfully lonely," I say. "Nobody should be lonely on Christmas Day."

He nods thoughtfully. "I'll have another word with your aunt. Maybe she'll relent." He adds a little sarcastically, "After all, she was full of talk about being charitable on Thanksgiving."

How well I remember! It was after dinner. Junior, my oldest cousin, was bemoaning the fact that they didn't have an automobile. All of his friends' families did. Even the DeLuccas, their neighbors, had just bought themselves a new Ford Victoria.

"Never mind your friends' families. And I don't care about the DeLuccas," Aunt Mary Margaret had said. "Just thank the Lord for what you *have* got. There's many would give a lot to be in your shoes."

Uncle Walter said, "This is Thanksgiving—a day to count your blessings instead of bellyaching about the luxuries you don't have. There's a depression on, you know."

Aunt Mary Margaret said, "You kids have too much already. You should learn to think of others."

I wondered if the "others" included the lazy, undeserving poor.

Then she turned to Maureen. "That reminds me—did you clean out your closet the way I told you to?"

Maureen nodded. "I put what I didn't want in a shopping bag."

"Then go get it. I'll bet Lizzie will be only too glad to take what you can't wear."

Papa said quickly, "Oh, don't bother."

I knew he hated to see me take hand-me-downs. I

wasn't quite as proud as he, though. I figured I deserved something good for putting up with a cousin like uppity Maureen.

When she returned with her castoffs, Aunt Mary Margaret started going through the bag. The first thing she pulled out was a blue and green plaid dress that looked pretty good. As I was picturing myself in it, she said, "What's this doing in here?"

"I don't like it," Maureen said.

"You don't like it!" Aunt Mary Margaret cried. "Why, you've hardly worn it."

"And I'm not going to. I hate it." Maureen grabbed the dress and pointed to the skirt. "See that—it's got a rip in it."

Aunt Mary Margaret examined the tear. "A needle and thread—if you could ever bring yourself to use them—would fix that easily enough. Oh no, you're not throwing this out. It's much too good."

The blue and green plaid went into a much-too-good pile. Aunt Mary Margaret then went through the rest of the clothes, item by item. Everything worth having joined the much-too-good pile. Everything not worth having went back into the shopping bag—all mine.

As we were about to leave, I whispered to Papa, "Nobody could wear this stuff. It's nothing but rags. Do I have to take it?"

Papa said, "You'll hurt your aunt's feelings if you don't."

I'd wondered then why it was that Aunt Mary Margaret's feelings were always the only ones that seemed to matter.

Now as I think about all this, I say to him, "I don't believe Aunt Mary Margaret will relent about having Grandpa Jake."

Papa says, "Her bark is always worse than her bite. Besides, it's Christmas, a time for forgiveness. I'll remind her of that."

"But what if she doesn't forgive? Then we'd have to stay home with Grandpa Jake, wouldn't we?" I say hopefully.

Papa gives a little sad smile. "Jake's never thought tradition very important himself. That's why Mary Margaret *does.*" Then he adds what I've come to feel is the same old tune. "We wouldn't want to hurt her feelings."

❄ 11 ❄

Preparing for
Our Grand Christmas

It is the next day after school. Cissy and I are in the kitchen with Grandpa Jake, having a fine time popping corn. I have not yet told her about quitting dance class because I mean to save it for a Christmas surprise.

Grandpa Jake shows us both how to string the popcorn. Although it is a tricky job, we soon have strand after strand, all ready to drape like tinsel around a tree.

"Sure there's nothin' that'll look more like snow," he says.

As we busy ourselves in the kitchen, Papa is at his job. I daydream that he will make so much money that he will never again have that worried look on his face when he says, "We just can't afford it."

As our handiwork piles up, we place it carefully in a cardboard carton that Grandpa Jake has picked up at the A&P store. He says, "When we finish the popcorn, we'll start stringin' cranberries. There's nothin' makes a prettier tree than popcorn and cranberries."

"I know how to make snowflakes from paper cutouts," I say. "Maybe we could hang those too."

"And why not, I'd like to know," Grandpa Jake says with a big smile. "There, now, you see what grand ornaments you can fashion with just a bit of imagination? Better than anythin' from some fancy emporium."

"Lizzie's friend, Tessie, says she's going to have gingerbread men on her tree this year," Cissy says.

I remember how fascinated Cissy was when Tess told us how her family always decorates with ornaments you can eat, like homemade candy or gingerbread men.

Grandpa Jake says, "Gingerbread men, is it? Well, now, we should be able to manage somethin' like that. A little Christmas bakin' is in order anyhow, I'm thinkin'."

"We'll need flour and sugar and things like that," I say, wondering what Papa will think of spending extra money.

"No problem," he says. "Ah, when I was a lad—" and for the rest of the afternoon he is off on stories of Christmases he remembers in the old country.

Later, when Papa comes home, he says, "Smells awful good in here."

"It's popcorn," I tell him, and show him all the long, fluffy white strands we have ready. "Grandpa Jake showed us how to make them."

"We strung cranberries too," Cissy says, then goes on to quote Grandpa Jake. "Nothing makes a prettier tree than popcorn and cranberries."

Papa frowns. "You know we don't bother with a tree, Lizzie. It would just be wasted when we go to your aunt's for Christmas."

"I know," I say. "But just in case."

The bedroom Cissy and I share is small and off the kitchen. Papa wants us to sleep there because our New England winters are so cold. We, at least, get a little warmth at night from the banked fire of the coal stove. Papa's bedroom is farthest from the kitchen. He now shares it with Grandpa Jake, who says it is an icebox. If we want to warm the whole house, we have to burn the small stove in the front room. Papa says that is only for special occasions.

Tonight Cissy is asleep, but I am restless. As Papa and Grandpa Jake play gin rummy at the kitchen table, I hear Papa say, "Jake, I appreciate all the time you're giving the girls, but I wish you'd stop putting ideas into their heads."

"Ideas, is it?" Grandpa Jake says. "Well, now, I've been meanin' to talk to you about that very subject. The girls want their Christmas at home. Like me, they are. I was never much for mixin' with a bunch of relations."

Papa, sounding impatient, says, "You don't understand, Jake. They get something at Mary Margaret's that they wouldn't get here. There's family and all the trimmings, including a big Christmas dinner, which I could never handle."

"Complete with your mama's plum puddin', is it?"

"Well, yes . . ."

Grandpa Jake chuckles. "No wonder the girls want to stay home."

Papa doesn't chuckle with him. "That's not the point. The point is the girls are learning about tradition there. I wouldn't know how to begin to teach them that."

"Well, now, the last thing I want to do is tell you how to raise your own kids. Seems to me, though, that tradition could do just as well without your dear mama's plum puddin'. God rest her soul, she had no talent for the kitchen."

I can hear the smile in Papa's voice as he says, "Neither does Mary Margaret. Nor, for that matter, do I."

"Then it's a lucky thing I do. I'll be doin' a bit of Christmas bakin' for the girls. Maybe I can teach them a little somethin' about tradition, too."

Grandpa Jake goes on talking about the ingredients he'll need. Papa tells him to pick them up at the neighborhood store and put the cost on our bill. Then I keep waiting for Grandpa Jake to tell Papa about the presents we want so badly, but soon they return to their gin rummy, and there is no more mention of Christmas. Before I go to sleep, I tell myself that Grandpa Jake is just being smart. He will wait until Papa is in a better mood.

❄ 12 ❄

Grandpa Jake
Telephones Santa

The next day, before Cissy and Grandpa Jake are up, Papa says to me, "As soon as I get a chance, I'll talk to your aunt about Jake. I think I can make her see the light."

Papa is ready for work, but he pauses in the kitchen to tell me this. I hope he is wrong. All I can think of is what a lovely holiday we could have at home with Grandpa Jake. An invitation to spend a merry Christmas at Aunt Mary Margaret's is always more of a threat than a promise.

When I say nothing in answer to Papa, he says, "I should be through with this job in a few days. Next week is the week before Christmas. You and Cissy will have to help me shop for gifts for your cousins."

I nod. We always wait until the last moment so that

Papa will know how much he can afford to spend.

Later that day I walk home with Tess, who is in my homeroom in junior high. (Cissy still goes to the elementary school near us.) I have been sharing my problems with Tess forever, so I say, "Cissy is counting on getting that Little Orphan Annie doll, and I don't think Grandpa Jake said anything to Papa about it."

"I'll bet that's because your grandfather will buy it himself," Tess says.

I have not seen Grandpa Jake spend any of his own money, so that has not occurred to me. The more I think about it, though, the more sense it makes. After all, he has gone out of his way to find out what we want. "I think you're right," I say to Tess, feeling better now.

Tess says, "Gee whiz, I sure wish you could stay home for Christmas. Then we could get together after dinner."

That is another reason why I hate to go to Aunt Mary Margaret's. I can never spend time with my best friend on the most important day of the year. I will have to give her her present, a beautiful bookmark I am making, on the day before or the day after. There's no holiday spirit that way.

"It's not really definite what we'll do yet," I say. "My father still has to talk to my aunt. I bet she won't have my grandfather, though. Not after the way she carried on about him."

"Your pa wouldn't just go off and leave him all by himself, would he?"

I shrug. "It all depends on whose feelings Papa thinks are more important. Of course, my aunt has her whole family. Grandpa Jake has only us. That should count a lot."

"Then there's still a chance. Oh, I hope you stay home."

"Me too. That's why I haven't said anything to Cissy yet."

I part from Tess in front of her house. As I cross the street, I see my sister waiting for me on the front stoop.

"Hurry up, Lizzie," she calls. "Grandpa Jake's going to help us make cookies. He's got all the 'gredients ready."

As I join her, she takes my hand, ready to pull me inside. "Wait a minute, Cissy," I say. "I want to talk to you first."

She pauses obediently, but I can see she is impatient to go where the real excitement is. "It'll only take a minute. It's important."

I have used the magic words. *It's important* is our code for something serious to come. Whether she says it or I say it, we have agreed that it means *Stop everything and listen!* Cissy gives me her full attention now.

I say, "Cissy, I don't want you to be too disappointed if we have to go to Aunt Mary Margaret's for Christmas."

She looks at me as if I am out of touch, but she will soon set me right. "Didn't you hear Grandpa Jake, Lizzie? He says we're going to have our own Christmas."

"That's not what he said. He said we ought to. There's a difference. Besides, it's not up to him. It's up to Papa."

Again she looks at me as if I am the world's biggest dummy. "Lizzie, Lizzie," she says, sounding like an old woman. "Don't you always tell me we have to do what Papa says?"

"Of course."

"Then Papa has to do what his papa says, too. And Grandpa Jake says we stay—"

"Oh, Cissy, it just doesn't work that way," I begin, then see the stubborn set of her jaw and realize she is not about to listen to anything I have to say. Besides, how do you reason with a seven-going-on-eight-year-old who has already reasoned the whole thing out for herself?

I make a last attempt. "Grandpa Jake said it would snow too—remember? And it hasn't."

"But it will. He said by Christmas Eve, and it isn't Christmas Eve yet."

Then Cissy pulls me down to her level and whispers in my ear, "Grandpa Jake told Santa about the Little Orphan Annie doll. And about the pink sweater too. Not exactly in person, though. He had to telephone him from the phone at the drugstore. The operator put him right through to the North Pole because he was such a good friend of Santa's."

That sounded like Grandpa Jake, all right. At least he hadn't forgotten our shopping trip. Tess must be right about his plans to buy the gifts himself. I am so relieved—not so much for myself but for Cissy. Everything hits you so much harder at that age.

I have finally decided on what to give Cissy for Christmas. With Mrs. Hanlon's help, I am crocheting a collar to turn one of her everyday dresses into a party dress. I think, too, I will tell her on Christmas Day that she can quit dancing class. I'll write it on a card that I'll box and tie with ribbon saved from last year. That way she'll have two presents from me. It's more fun to have lots of boxes to open.

✻ 13 ✻

Cissy and Dancing School

For the rest of the week, Grandpa Jake spends every afternoon with Cissy and me, baking good things for Christmas. At night he is off to visit his old friend. No matter how much we see of him, we still miss him when he's gone.

With borrowed cookie cutters and pans, we have been turning out gingerbread men with smiling icing faces and all kinds of other cookies, some with candied cherries and anise, some full of raisins and nuts, and others speckled with pretty colored sugars. With all the spices and flavorings, our kitchen has never smelled better.

Grandpa Jake even knows how to make fruitcake. At first Cissy turned up her nose when he suggested it.

"That's that old dark cake with all those green lumps in it," she complained.

Grandpa Jake soon cured her of that idea. His fruitcake is not dark but white. And the lumps are yellow pineapple instead of green citron. It is delicious. What's more, he lets us help with everything so that we can make some of these things ourselves in the future. What a good time we have, mixing, baking, testing, and writing down his recipes. Then we store everything away in the airtight tins that Mama once used, all ready for the big day.

By the following week I have all of my Christmas gifts ready except something for Grandpa Jake. I have finished Papa's pot-holder mitten, Tess's bookmark, and Cissy's collar. Because Grandpa Jake is such a good cook, I decide to make him a pot-holder mitten too. There is still time.

I make my decision as I hurry home from school to pick up Cissy and head for dancing class. She takes only one lesson a week, on Mondays. I take three, although right now I am going every day to rehearse for the Christmas program. As we near Main Street, I keep wondering when I should tell Papa about my idea for continuing lessons. After my *Nutcracker* performance, I think. That should be the perfect time, when he sees what a serious dancer I am. As for Cissy, he knows her teacher says she shows no interest, so it won't matter if she quits and I go on.

I say to her now, "I know how much you hate dancing school, but—"

She breaks in. "Oh no, Lizzie. I don't hate dancing school. I *love* it!"

I think I must be hearing wrong. "But just a little while ago you didn't like it."

"I do now. You want to know why?"

I begin to feel a tinge of uneasiness. "Why?"

"Because Ruthie and I are practicing our military tap real hard. You want to know why?"

"Why?" I say stiffly.

"Because Art Patchen says if we do good, we can be in the next recital."

"But you can't be in the recital unless you know the whole dance from beginning to end. And you have to be as good as everybody else."

"Ruthie and I are going to be better than everybody else. We're going to be the best," she says staunchly. "You want to know why?"

"Yes."

"Because we're best friends, that's why."

"But that doesn't mean—" I start to say, then close my mouth. What difference does it make? This is not what I was expecting at all. I remind myself that Cissy is only seven, and seven-year-olds change their minds from day to day.

As usual, I help with Cissy's class until Art gets there. While I show one of the boys a time step, I keep glancing over to Cissy. She and Ruthie, side by side, holding hands, are tapping through as much of their military tap routine as they know. They still have a long way to go, but I have to admit they have both improved. Every so often Cissy takes her eyes from her feet to glance at Ruthie. At the same time Ruthie looks at her, and they exchange pleased-with-themselves grins. Maybe the lessons are doing Cissy some good after all.

Even so, I tell myself, mine are more important. Cissy's recital is only a short-term goal. She doesn't even know what long-term goals are. And, anyhow, what purpose will it serve if we both leave dancing school? No, it will have to be Cissy. It just can't mean as much to her as it does to me.

That night, when Cissy is in bed and Grandpa Jake is out visiting his old friend, Papa says to me, "I looked in on Cissy's teacher this afternoon."

"Why?" I ask, puzzled. Usually Papa never goes near school unless there's a serious reason.

"Well, I've been worried about Cissy. When her teacher talked to me before, she made it sound as though Cissy had some kind of sickness or something."

"Tess's little brother is in Cissy's class. Tess says the teacher is new—just out of normal school. I don't think she's very used to kids. Cissy just needs time. She'll do better when she's ready."

"That's just it. She tells me Cissy *is* doing better. She's starting to talk more to the other kids and is raising her hand once in a while. I guess you're right, Lizzie. Cissy just needs time." As an afterthought, he says, "You don't suppose those dancing lessons have anything to do with it, do you?"

I think of Cissy tapping away, holding Ruthie's hand, and I find myself avoiding his eyes. "If you want to know what I think, I think that teacher just doesn't know there are different kinds of kids in the world and that some kids, like Cissy, are naturally shy. I think that teacher just likes to cause trouble."

"Oh, I'm sure she didn't mean to do that," Papa assures me. "But I must say I'm relieved to hear Cissy's improving. I can stand some good news."

Who couldn't? I think.

❋ 14 ❋

Heaven's the Place
for Martyrs

Grandpa Jake and I are alone in the kitchen this afternoon. Papa is out buying groceries for supper, and Cissy is at the Hanlons' next door. At last I have a chance to again share my worries with someone who understands.

I say, "Grandpa Jake, remember what we talked about the other day?" When he looks at me blankly, I quickly add, "I mean, about quitting dancing class and all."

"Oh, that. Well, now, I thought we'd put our two heads together and solved that problem."

"So did I. But that was when I thought Cissy didn't like taking lessons. Now she says she loves it." I tell him about my conversation with her and about her teacher in school saying she is improving. Trying to be fair, I add, "If it's the lessons that are helping her, maybe it would be wrong to make her give them up."

He mulls over my words, then says, "Maybe your papa will see fit to let the two of you keep on."

"No, he won't," I say firmly, wondering why Grandpa Jake would even suggest that after all I have told him. I hope it isn't because he is trying to dismiss the subject because it is so unimportant. I mean, with the Depression and so many people out of work, my problems may seem silly to a grownup.

He relieves my mind when he goes right to the heart of the situation. "As I see it, what it comes down to then is you have to make a choice. It's you or Cissy."

Exactly. I nod sadly and wait for him to find the right words to solve my dilemma, as I am sure he will. I am not disappointed.

Grandpa Jake says, "Would you be the same young lady who agreed with me that life would have no meanin' without a dream?"

Indeed, I was. "Yes, but that was before I knew about Cissy."

"God love you, Cissy's a baby—too young for dreams of her own."

"That's true," I agree. After all, Cissy's are only short, not long-term goals. That should make a difference.

"And if the lessons have done her good, well, then, they've served their purpose, wouldn't you say?"

"I guess so."

"I've always said, darlin', if there's somethin' you want badly enough, there's always a way to get it. And it's not by makin' a martyr out of yourself. Sometimes you've got to fight for what you want." He gives me his big, mischievous grin. "I never did think much of martyrs anyhow. Some say they come from heaven. I say that's the place for them, and they should stay there."

I am so glad I talked to him. I know now that my feelings can be trusted. What's more, I know why. I can see there is nothing worse than acting like a martyr, which is what I would be doing. I decide to talk to Papa immediately instead of waiting until after *The Nutcracker* performance.

My chance comes that night when Grandpa Jake is out visiting and Cissy is in bed. As Papa banks the kitchen coal stove for the night, I look up from my homework and say, "Papa, I need to talk to you."

He stops what he is doing and glances over to me, eyebrows raised. "About what?"

"About dancing lessons."

"Lizzie, I thought we'd gone all through that."

"Yes, but I want to ask you something."

He shrugs. "Ask away."

I swallow hard. "If Miss Pontchartrain hadn't raised the price, would you have let Cissy and me continue?"

"I don't know. I hadn't really thought about it. I suppose so."

Then I was right. It was only the increase he was worried about. "If there was a way that it wouldn't cost more, would it be all right?"

"All right to continue your lessons?"

I nod.

Instead of answering my question, he says, "Lizzie—mind you, I'm not complaining—but with your grandfather here, it takes more money to live."

"I know," I persist, "but would you have let us keep on if it didn't cost more?"

He considers my words and sighs. "Probably."

That is all I am waiting for. I say quickly, "If Cissy quits—and you know she didn't want to take lessons in the first place—then it won't cost a penny more than it did."

He looks at me thoughtfully, then says, "I don't know. I don't want to do anything that isn't fair. Still, if she isn't showing any interest, the way her teacher said, then"—he throws up his hands—"why not?"

I don't like to think about the "showing interest" part because she *is,* but I remember what Grandpa Jake and I have talked about. Sometimes you have to fight for what you want. "I think she'd like to quit," I say, not looking at him.

He says again, "Well, I just want to be fair. I know how much this means to you, Lizzie, but I thought it might be helping Cissy, too. If it isn't, you might as well keep on, at least until we can't manage anymore."

"Thank you, Papa," I say.

"I'll tell Cissy."

I *should* feel like pirouetting all around the room. Somehow, I don't.

* 15 *

A Place of Sunshine
and Riches

Tomorrow is the big night. Aunt Mary Margaret says none of her family will be coming to see me dance in *The Nutcracker* because they are entertaining Uncle Walter's folks that night. I think that is just an excuse because she doesn't want to see Grandpa Jake. I don't care, though. I'd rather have him.

I have spent the afternoon at dress rehearsal, which went really well. Lucky for me I fit into the Sugar Plum Fairy costume Mabel Dennis wore last year. Papa could never have afforded a new one. Miss Pontchartrain must know that. This is not the first time she has helped me that way.

I am all excited as I come home, itching to talk about what a wonderful night it will be, what a wonderful performance. I promise myself to make Papa and Grandpa Jake proud of me.

It is almost time for supper. I find Papa alone in the kitchen, stirring a pot on the stove. Yesterday was his last day on the job. "Where's Cissy?" I ask him.

He gestures with his head toward his bedroom. "Helping Jake pack."

Pack? I don't really understand. "What's he packing?"

"His things, of course."

For a moment I don't know what to say. Then I ask, "Why?"

Papa sounds distant, almost as if this has nothing to do with him, as he says, "Ask him."

I hurry to Papa's room, where Grandpa Jake is folding away his belongings into the satchel he came with. Cissy, not saying a word, is watching his every move. Surely he can't be leaving us for good. Not now. Not before my performance. Not before Christmas.

"What are you doing, Grandpa Jake?" I ask.

He pauses and looks up at me. "Ah, Elizabeth, darlin' . . . It's sad that I'm goin' to have to miss your lovely show."

"But I was counting on you." I still cannot believe there isn't some mistake. "I thought you'd be here."

"And I was thinkin' the same thing myself until yesterday."

"What happened yesterday?" I demand.

He ignores my question to continue in his own way. "Sure I'd like nothin' better than to see my own granddaughter dance like the angel she is"—he sighs sadly—"but when an old friend needs help"—he shrugs—"what can you do?"

"What kind of help?" I say, growing impatient with his roundabout way of explaining things.

"Now, now, all in good time." He shakes his head good-naturedly. "Like your sainted grandma, you are, always wantin' quick answers to complicated questions."

But I am not like my sainted grandma. He himself has told me I am like him.

"Well, now," he continues, "it's like this . . ." He takes a long time telling us about his old friend and about how many years they've known each other and how, in the old days, his friend—like kin, they were—had done him untold favors. The story goes on and on and is, indeed, complicated. I can't follow half of it. The part I do follow isn't at all complicated. His friend has a son in Florida and goes there every year for Christmas.

"Wants me to help with the drivin'," Grandpa Jake finally says. "Big Packard tourin' car, it is, and a joy to travel in. Seems the least I can do for someone who's done me many a good turn. A person needs someone to spell them on a long trip like that."

"I didn't know you could drive," I say. Hardly anyone I know owns a car, let alone drives one.

"Oh, I've tried my hand at it a couple of times. I figure what I don't know I'll pick up along the way. On the job trainin', you might say."

75

"Are you coming back for Christmas?" Cissy asks anxiously.

"Mind you, there's nothin' I'd like better. But it's a far distance, darlin'. Besides, you and Elizabeth and your pa won't even be here. You'll be havin' a fine time for yourselves at your aunt Mary Margaret's. You'll never even miss me."

So that's why he's leaving, I think. Aunt Mary Margaret won't have him for Christmas and neither will Papa. How could you blame anyone for not staying where he wasn't wanted? Still, he might have postponed the trip for just a day to see *The Nutcracker* . . .

Grandpa Jake gives a wistful smile. "Ah, many's the fortune that's been made in Florida. A place of sunshine and riches, it is. Who knows? If I like it there, I may stay." He pulls Cissy to him and gives her a big hug. "When you get tired of the snow, your pa can bring you to visit. What a time we'll have, pickin' oranges and grapefruit right off the trees. Och, it's that excited I am I can hardly think straight."

He goes on talking about the wonders of Florida. For a moment I forget my feelings of betrayal. I am caught up in his enthusiasm. He almost has Cissy and me feeling that we are going, too, and that soon our lives will be showered with the same sunshine and riches.

He is to stay the night at his friend's house, he tells us, so that they can get an early start in the morning.

It is only after we kiss him good-bye and he has left for the bus that our reaction sets in.

In spite of all that talk about sunshine, Cissy says, "Does it snow for Christmas in Florida? I like snow for Christmas." Her eyes swim with tears.

❄16❄

I Make Papa Mad

It is the evening of the day Grandpa Jake has left us. Cissy is in bed. Papa is playing solitaire at the kitchen table. I am trying to read, but my mind keeps wandering. Even though lately Grandpa Jake has been spending his nights visiting, the house seems lonely without him. Like when Mama died.

I am about to go to bed when Papa says, "After school on Monday you and Cissy and I will go over town and see what we can buy for your cousins. Do you know what they want?"

Oh, yes, I know. At least I know what Maureen wants—angora mittens and beret. Papa never asks what Cissy and I want. It is always what do we most need? Instead of answering him, I find myself saying, "You don't miss him at all, do you?"

He looks at me strangely. "Miss who? Jake?"

I nod.

Papa gives a twisty smile. "I'm used to Jake's ways."

I think Papa is acting icy cold when he should be sad like Cissy and me. "It's your fault, you know," I blurt out. I have never talked to Papa like that before, but I just can't seem to stop myself.

"What's my fault?"

"You were going to leave Grandpa Jake all alone for Christmas. That's why he left. How could you do that?"

Papa frowns. "Is that what he told you?"

I start to say yes, then think back and realize he didn't actually say those words. "He might just as well have. That's what you were going to do—leave him alone. And I think that's mean."

"Lizzie, you don't know what you're talking about. I saw your aunt this morning and talked her into having him. And a fat lot of use that was. When I got home, he was already packing his things."

I still wanted to blame someone. "Well, you waited too long. He just didn't feel wanted. If we could have had Christmas at home, I bet he wouldn't have gone to Florida with that man."

"I don't believe I could have done anything that would have made him miss a trip like that. And it wasn't a man, by the way, it was a woman."

A woman? I guess I just assumed Grandpa Jake's old friend would be a man. "What woman?"

"The wife of someone Jake knew from the days

when he sold insurance. The man—well insured, I'll bet—died about six months ago." Papa gave a wry smile. "Apparently Jake's been consoling the widow. It wouldn't surprise me if that was his reason for coming here in the first place."

I think about that. How could Grandpa Jake believe that some old widow was more important than Cissy and me? "He said she wanted him to drive her to Florida, and he owed her a favor."

"I don't know about the favor, but the driving part is true enough. As I understand it, she planned to spend Christmas with her son. The Packard was her husband's car. She wanted her son to have it, and Jake came up with this way of getting it to him."

"But she was the one who asked Grandpa Jake."

Papa rolled his eyes. "I have no doubt she believes that as sincerely as you do."

"You're saying that Grandpa Jake tells lies to people!"

Papa sighs. "No, that's not what I'm saying. It's just that he has a way of making people accept his ideas as their own."

I look at him doubtfully. "I bet you're making this up out of your imagination just because you want to think bad about him."

"Oh, Lizzie, I stopped thinking bad of Jake years ago. Jake is Jake. And there's a lot of good in him. If you can just take him the way he is without expecting more, your life can be a lot richer for it."

I don't really understand that. All I know is Cissy

and I have placed our trust in him and, if I can believe Papa, he has let us down.

Papa says, "Anyhow, he's gone, and we have to get on with the business of our own lives. On Monday we'll go shopping the way we planned."

Shopping for our cousins. It's bad enough that Grandpa Jake doesn't think Cissy and I are important. It's worse that Papa doesn't. I find myself saying, "At least Grandpa Jake wouldn't have made us go to Aunt Mary Margaret's for Christmas. He knows how much we hate it."

"Hate? That's a pretty strong word." Papa smiles.

"Oh, you're not even listening. You never take me seriously. And I don't care if it is a strong word. That's how we feel—both of us."

"But, Lizzie, you're old enough to understand that I'm only trying to do what's best for you and Cissy."

Now that I have started, I can't stop. "No, you're not. If you were, you'd let us stay home."

"But it wouldn't be nearly as nice. I couldn't do all the things your aunt does."

"We don't care about that," I say stubbornly.

"They're family, Lizzie. Families always get together that time of year. Besides, your aunt's just trying to give you a sense of tradition, something you'll remember all your life."

"But we're a family, too—you and me and Cissy. And what good is tradition anyhow if all you remember is how awful Christmas was every year? I don't see why we can't make our own tradition."

Papa shakes his head hopelessly. "I wish it were different, but after we buy your cousins' presents, there won't be enough money left to have what amounts to a second Christmas here."

"If we can't afford it, then why do we have to buy them presents at all? You blame Grandpa Jake for not caring about his family. Well, I think you're just like him then. You care more about Aunt Mary Margaret's family than you do about us."

Papa looks stunned. "That's not true. Besides, I never said Jake didn't care about his family. He does—in his own way and if it doesn't take a lot of effort on his part. If anything, he's irresponsible."

"Well, maybe there are other ways of being irresponsible. Like not paying any attention to what your own kids want."

"When haven't I paid attention to you?" he demands indignantly. "I've let you continue your lessons, haven't I? Which reminds me, I haven't mentioned it to Cissy yet, but I will."

I am still angry. Ever since yesterday when Grandpa Jake left us, I have this awful knot inside me that just won't untangle. "Even so," I say, "when you gave all the good things to Aunt Mary Margaret's family last Christmas and long underwear to Cissy and me, you weren't thinking of us."

"I thought you would understand."

"Well, we don't." I feel my eyes smart. "And this year, when Cissy doesn't get the doll she's expecting, she's going to be heartbroken." There is something besides the doll that may make her feel just as bad, but I don't want to think about that.

"What doll?" he says.

I guess I wasn't really surprised that he didn't know. I tell him about the day we shopped with Grandpa Jake, about the Little Orphan Annie doll, and about the pink sweater and single strand of pearls. "He practically promised us we'd get them for Christmas. Then he must have forgotten all about it. He even told Cissy he'd telephoned Santa Claus and it was all set."

Papa's face reddens now. I am suddenly frightened that I have gone too far and made him very angry. "Blast Jake!" He slams his fist on the table. "Him and his silver tongue. Oh, I should have known he'd never change. Up to his old tricks as usual. He had no right to come here and disrupt our lives."

"But he did," I murmur.

Papa looks at me as if he hardly sees me and says, "Go to bed, Lizzie."

Without another word, I obey. I have never seen him so mad.

Sleep won't come, though. As I listen to Cissy's even breathing, all I can think of is how Grandpa Jake has hurt us and how there is still another hurt in store for her.

❄17❄

Good-Bye to Clara

I am the last one in the dressing room, changing from my costume to my everyday clothes. The other kids are already on their way out to join their parents. I can hear them through the door, laughing and chattering, all excited about the performance that had gone even better than dress rehearsal.

Although I had little heart for my role tonight, I remembered how Miss Pontchartrain always reminded us that great performers never let their personal troubles show. It is not professional. I think I can say that, in spite of the knot that is still inside me, I was professional.

All day long I have been thinking about Grandpa Jake and about how much I hate him. Well, not him exactly but what he did. He'd just about had me believing he was some kind of fairy godfather who could make my dearest wishes come true. Maybe he hadn't deliberately deceived us about everything. But maybe it's worse to make promises so lightly that you don't even take them seriously yourself. And with no thought to how much you hurt others. Now I am one of those others, and I know how bad it feels.

Papa says Grandpa Jake has a silver tongue. I would call it tinsel.

I am just about ready to join Cissy and Papa when Miss Pontchartrain peers in the door, a surprised look on her face. "You're still here, Elizabeth. What's taking you so long?"

I say, "I guess I'm just slow." I don't tell her I have been hoping to see her alone. I know what I must do now, but it is hard.

She beams at me. "You were a wonderful Sugar Plum Fairy. In fact, everyone gave a first-rate performance tonight. Of course, Mabel lost it a few times, and her style is something less than heartfelt, but I don't think the audience really noticed. I suppose we have to expect a few mistakes from nervousness."

She continues, her practiced eye zeroing in on everyone's errors. All the while I am thinking I would not have made any mistakes as Clara, and my performance *would* have been heartfelt.

She says, "Oh well, all and all, it was a decent presentation, and you were very nearly perfect."

That is such high praise it makes it even harder to get out what I have to say.

"I have some new ideas for next year. Of course you'll dance Clara."

The big knot inside me feels as if it has crept up to my throat now. With difficulty I say, "I don't think I can."

Her forehead wrinkles with a confused frown. "I don't understand."

"I mean, I can't. I can't be Clara or anything else. In fact, I'll be leaving the school next week."

"Leaving? Why? Are you moving away?"

"Oh, no." I try to change the subject. "Cissy will still be here. She's enjoying her lessons now, and they're really doing her lots of good." In fact, I mean to tell Papa just how much good. It was wrong of me to keep that to myself.

"I still want to know why *you're* leaving. You're one of my best pupils."

I remember how Papa hates for people to know we are, as he puts it, up against it. I shrug and try to sound happier than I feel. "I've had years of lessons. I just think it's time to do something else. I'm a little tired of dancing anyhow."

"I didn't know that," she says thoughtfully. "You've always been so enthusiastic."

"Yes, well . . ." I am saved from explaining further when Cissy comes tearing into the dressing room, looking so disturbed I don't think she even notices I am not alone.

She cries, "Papa says I can't take tap anymore because I don't want to, but I do want to, and he doesn't

86

believe me. You gotta tell him, Lizzie." She grabs my hand and tries to pull me along with her.

I turn back to Miss Pontchartrain with an apologetic smile. "I'd better go." As I follow my sister out of the room, I say, "Calm down, Cissy. It's all right. You'll still be taking tap."

She slows her steps and says hopefully, "I will?"

"Yes, you will. Papa just didn't know that you like tap. He thought he was doing you a favor, letting you quit."

"Oh, I do like tap. I love tap."

"I know. I'll tell him, and it'll be all right."

From the look of relief on Cissy's face, I know I have done the right thing. The knot inside me begins to untangle, but a big cold emptiness takes its place.

How I hate being a martyr! Yet there is still something worse—being like Grandpa Jake.

❄ 18 ❄

Saved!

By the following day my martyrdom sits even heavier on my shoulders than it did last night when I told Papa my decision.

"But I thought you were wild about dancing," he'd said.

"I thought so too for a while, but I guess I'm really not," I answered.

Then he rolled his eyes and threw up his hands. "Girls! I'll never understand them. Well, if that's really the way you feel, so be it. I suppose you can always go back if you change your mind and things start looking up."

Papa just doesn't realize about ballet. It can't be an on-again, off-again thing. Besides, things are never going to start *looking up*. I spend that day, a gloomy

Sunday, with my nose in a book, not taking in a word.

On Monday after school, while Papa and I are waiting for Cissy to get home, he says, "We'll drop your sister off at dancing school this afternoon. While she's having her lesson, you and I will go Christmas shopping. Are you ready?"

"I guess," I say without enthusiasm.

"Now what have I done?" He exclaims in an injured voice that makes me feel ashamed.

I have had time to think about how brazen I was to him, accusing him of thinking more of Aunt Mary Margaret's family than of us. I remember how angry he was when I finished. I don't want to make things worse. "You haven't done anything. And I'm ready to go shopping if you are." Then I add, "I know what Maureen wants—angora mittens and a—"

"Never mind Maureen. We won't be exchanging presents. I told your aunt this morning that we can't afford it this year."

He actually told Aunt Mary Margaret? And even admitted we couldn't afford it?! "I can't believe it," I say without thinking.

"I know." He doesn't sound offended. "I guess when I thought about it, I wasn't crazy about having one of my kids accuse me of being like Jake. Which doesn't mean that I don't care about him. I do. I just don't care much for what he does."

I felt the same. "What did Aunt Mary Margaret say when you told her?"

"She said it was all Jake's doing, that she knew the

minute he came here he'd cause trouble." Papa gives a wry smile. "And you know something? She was right. But maybe some of it was the kind of trouble we needed."

I'm not sure what he means. I say, "If we aren't exchanging presents, what are we going shopping for?"

"For the doll, of course. And the sweater."

I am speechless. But not for long. "And the single strand of pearls?"

"*And* the single strand of pearls."

I still can't believe it. "Does that mean we're staying home for Christmas?"

"Yes, we're staying home. Such as it is, I guess we'll try to make our own tradition."

For a moment I don't utter a word. I wait. The sky doesn't fall. Lightning doesn't strike. Has all this come about simply because I spoke my mind?

Papa has left Cissy and me at dancing school and gone on to the five-and-ten, which is just up the street. I am to meet him there in twenty minutes. Inside the studio, Cissy heads for her class, and I go upstairs to pick up the few things I leave there for practice. I do not plan to return for the lessons that remain before year's end. They would only make me feel sad.

As I come down with my things, I just about bump into Miss Pontchartrain. Sounding agitated, she says, "Where have you been, Elizabeth?" She points to Cissy's room. "Art's been held up, and the kids are running wild in there. Hurry up and get changed and see what you can do with them."

I stare at her, thinking I must have dreamed Saturday night when I told her I was leaving this week. "I can't, Miss Pontchartrain. I have to meet my father to go Christmas shopping. Besides, I'm only here to pick up my things. I'm not coming back."

"Not coming back?" She sounds as if she has forgotten. Then she pauses a moment and obviously remembers. "Oh, yes," she says thoughtfully, looking the way she does when she is displeased. She glances toward Cissy's room. "Could you stay just until Art gets here? I have my hands full upstairs with beginner's ballet."

She doesn't even care that I'm leaving, I think. All that matters to her is making her own job easier. "I can't stay. I told my father I'd meet him," I say firmly. Then because I suddenly feel it doesn't matter what she thinks of me, I blurt out, "I don't see why you keep Art Patchen when he's late all the time!"

Her eyes widen. I expect her to tell me to mind my own business. Instead, she says, "It's not easy to find teachers as good as Art, especially for what I can pay. He does this because he loves it."

"But he has another job too."

"Yes, in a furniture store, but only part-time. He has to work both jobs to make ends meet. He's on commission there, so he can't afford to walk out in the middle of a sale. That's why he's late so often."

Making ends meet is an old story in my life, so I can feel sorry for him. "I didn't know."

Raucous screams, then laughter issue from Cissy's class. Miss Pontchartrain glances toward the room with an irritated expression, then up the stairs where her beginners wait. She says again, "Could you just stay for a few minutes, Elizabeth?"

I think of all the time I have spent with Cissy's class with never even a thank you from Miss Pontchartrain. Why should I care about helping her now? "Even if I stayed today, what will you do from now on when I'm not here?"

She looks at a loss. "Well, I don't know. . . . I'll have to make some other arrangement—something permanent, from the looks of it—maybe use one of the advanced students to assist."

With all the noise coming from Cissy's room now, I can see Miss Pontchartrain is too rattled at the moment to give the matter careful thought. Something Grandpa Jake said flashes through my mind. *If there's something you want badly enough, there's always a way to get it.* I say, "You'd have to pay an advanced student." I don't mention, of course, that I *am* an advanced student. "I mean, lots of times when I was working with my sister's class, I should have been practicing myself. It wouldn't be fair to ask someone to give up their own time for nothing." I have never done anything like this before, but what have I to lose?

Miss Pontchartrain stares at me as if I am some strange new person she has never seen before. I have the feeling she is ticking off in her head all the minutes I have spent in Cissy's class and adding them up. Finally, in a small voice, she says, "I can't pay very much."

I am far ahead of her now. "I'll bet the person would be glad to take it out in lessons."

I can almost hear a sigh of relief. "What a good idea!" She gives me a big smile. "Why don't you consider the job and get your own lessons free? After all, you're very good with children. Oh"—she pauses— "but you're tired of dancing."

I say quickly. "Not that tired. Besides, something like this would make it more interesting. I'd love the job."

"Wonderful. You're hired."

A loud yelp from Cissy's room is the sign that mayhem is about to break loose. Miss Pontchartrain says hurriedly, "We'll work out the details tomorrow. Right now, I beg you, go in there and do something with those kids."

I am only too glad to oblige, knowing Papa will come back to the studio when I don't meet him. By the time he does, Art has arrived and taken over.

As we head for the stores, I tell Papa all about the new job. "I'll even get my lessons free," I tell him.

"And you want to do this?"

"Of course, Papa."

He shakes his head, a little smile on his lips. "I can't keep up with all this now-you-will, now-you-won't business. I guess I just don't understand you, Lizzie."

I shrug. "Aunt Mary Margaret would say I've reached the awkward age," I offer. Then feeling very good and very brave, I venture, "From now on, Papa, I'd like it if you'd call me Elizabeth."

❋ 19 ❋

Christmas Day

It is Christmas Day. Yesterday afternoon Papa, Cissy, and I took a nice box of Grandpa Jake's cookies over to Aunt Mary Margaret's. She was surprised—I suppose because Papa had told her we wouldn't be exchanging gifts. She insisted we take a big bowl of her plum pudding.

On the bus ride home, Papa, balancing the dish awkwardly on his lap, said, "Well, at least this year we won't have to eat the darned stuff."

Cissy and I giggled.

A few minutes later I glanced out the window to find a light snow coming down. Excited, I said, "Look, Cissy, it's starting to snow."

She stared out the window and smiled. "Grandpa Jake said it would."

On Christmas Eve you can get holiday bargains for almost nothing, so last night Papa bought our tree. He also bought a gold angel for the top and a string of colored lights. "Next year we'll get another," he said.

Next year!

Papa, Cissy, and I stayed up late decorating the tree. Papa placed the lights. Cissy and I put on the popcorn and cranberry strands that Grandpa Jake helped us make. Then we added my snowflake cutouts and the gold angel.

The tree sat proudly in the front-room window, where everyone was sure to see it. When we turned on the lights and stood back to admire, I could have cried. It was beautiful.

Cissy, quoting Grandpa Jake, said, "Nothing makes a prettier tree than popcorn and cranberries."

Papa told us to hang our stockings and get to bed. We did, but we both spent a restless night.

This morning when we awoke, he had a fire going in the front-room stove. Our limp stockings were now bulging with apples, oranges, and Christmas hard candy. We nibbled some as we opened our presents.

Papa really crowed about the pot-holder mitten from Cissy and me. Of course I knew what I was getting. I had helped Papa pick it out—my lovely pink sweater and single strand of pearls. Still I acted surprised for Cissy's sake and gave Papa a big hug and kiss. My best present, though, is looking forward to my new role in dancing school and to dancing Clara in next year's *Nutcracker*.

Papa and I both enjoyed watching Cissy open the box with her Little Orphan Annie doll. She took so long untying the ribbon and was so cautious about lifting the lid that I wondered if she had just a moment of doubt. When she saw the doll, she slapped a palm over her mouth and gave a nervous giggle, so I think I was right.

"Look at the card," I said.

She stared at the words Papa had written: To Cissy from Santa Claus. Then a big smile lit her face and she said, "See, Papa, I told you Grandpa Jake knew Santa Claus."

It is afternoon now. We have already had dinner. Papa bought a small ham because it will go a long way. We had canned peas and jellied cranberry sauce with it. He had a baked sweet potato, which Cissy and I don't like. We had Franco-American spaghetti. For dessert we ate Grandpa Jake's fruitcake. Cissy and I agreed it was the best Christmas dinner we ever had.

Now I'm expecting Tess to come over. I can hardly wait to see her face when she sees the beautiful book-mark I have made for her. I know she will have one for me, too. It's the same thing we gave each other last Christmas. We are great readers, though, and wear them out fast.

I have thought and thought about Grandpa Jake and about Christmas. It seems to me that somehow, because of him, everything turned out just right. But I can't credit him with the snow. I'm sure that was just the luck of the Irish.

From all that happened, I suspect I have a lot of Grandpa Jake in me. I also have a lot of Papa, so maybe that makes it all right.

As I ponder this, the doorbell rings. Cissy runs to answer. I hear Tess's voice as she says, "Did you have a nice Christmas, Cissy?"

Cissy says, "Oh, yes, Tessie, we had a grand Christmas!"